Miss Brick the Builders' Baby

Ahlberg & McNaughton

PUFFIN

PUFFIN BOOKS

UK | USA | Canada | Ireland | Australia
India | New Zealand | South Africa

Puffin Books is part of the Penguin Random House group of companies
whose addresses can be found at global.penguinrandomhouse.com.

www.penguin.co.uk   www.puffin.co.uk   www.ladybird.co.uk

First published in hardback by Viking and in paperback by Puffin Books 1981
This edition published 2017

001

Text copyright © Allan Ahlberg, 1981
Illustrations copyright © Colin McNaughton, 1981
Educational Advisory Editor: Brian Thompson

The moral right of the author and illustrator has been asserted

Printed in China
A CIP catalogue record for this book is available from the British Library

ISBN: 978–0–141–37747–6

All correspondence to:
Puffin Books, Penguin Random House Children's
80 Strand, London WC2R 0RL

This is the house
that Mr and Mrs Brick built.
This is the baby
that lived in the house
that Mr and Mrs Brick built.
This is the story of that baby.

Mr and Mrs Brick were builders.
They had been builders all their lives.
Their mothers and fathers
had been builders.
Their grandmothers and grandfathers
had been builders.
There had been builders
in the Brick family for years
and years and years.

Archimedes
Brick

Bodicea
Brick

Norman Le Brick

Henry Brick

Sir Christopher
Brick

Isambard
Kingdom Brick

Angus McBrick

Patrick O'Brick

Great Uncle
Brick

So when Baby Brick was born,
Mr and Mrs Brick were very happy.
"Now we have another builder
in the family!" they said.
But did they really have
another builder in the family?
No, they did not.
Mr Brick was a builder.
Mrs Brick was a builder.
Baby Brick was *not* a builder

This is the house that Baby Brick . . .

. . . knocked down!

And this!

And this!

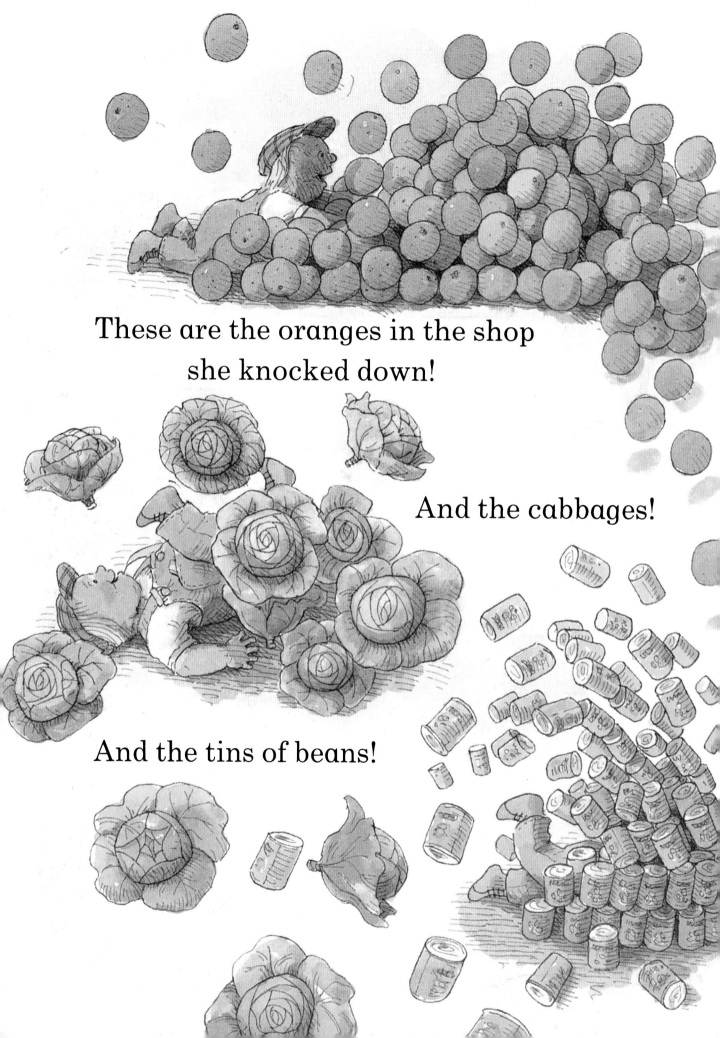

These are the oranges in the shop
she knocked down!

And the cabbages!

And the tins of beans!

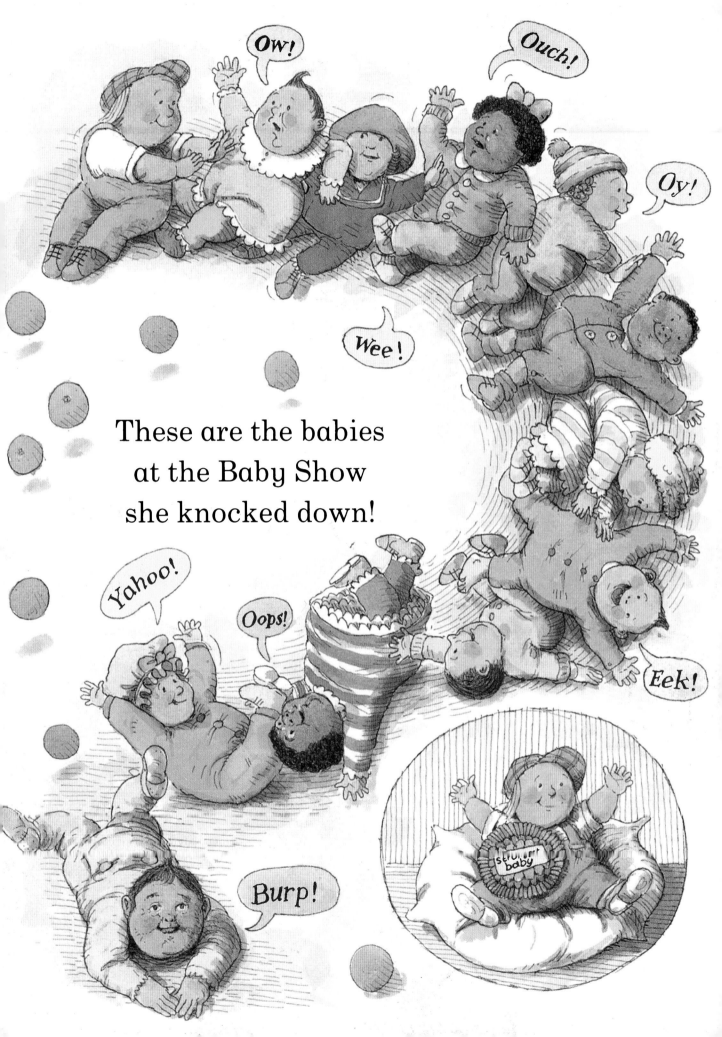

These are the babies
at the Baby Show
she knocked down!

Mr and Mrs Brick were worried.
They put Baby Brick in her carry-cot.
They went down the road
to see Auntie Brick.
"Our baby does not build,"
said Mr Brick.
"She knocks things down!"
Mrs Brick said.
Auntie stopped work
and put her glasses on.
She looked at the baby.
"What this baby needs is a pet,"
she said.
"It will take her mind off
knocking things down!"

So the next day Mr and Mrs Brick
bought a dog and built a dog konnel.
And was that the answer?

No, it was not.
Baby Brick loved the dog –
but knocked the dog-kennel down.

Mr and Mrs Brick bought two rabbits
and built a rabbit-hutch.
Baby Brick knocked the rabbit-hutch
down.

They bought four chickens
and built a chicken-house.
Baby Brick knocked
the chicken-house down.

Now Mr and Mrs Brick
were more worried.
They put Baby Brick in her pram.
They got on a bus
and went to another town
to see Grandma Brick.

"Our baby knocks things down,"
said Mrs Brick.
"She does not build a single thing!"
Mr Brick said.

Grandma stopped work
and made a pot of tea.
She looked at the baby.
"What this baby needs is a bit of fun,"
she said.
"It will take her mind off
knocking things down!"
So the next week Mr and Mrs Brick
had a party for Baby Brick.
And was that the answer?
No, it was not.
This is the trifle and jelly and cake . . .

 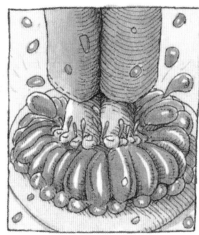 

. . . that Baby Brick knocked down.

Mr and Mrs Brick took Baby Brick
to the seaside.
This is the sand-castle
that Baby Brick knocked down.

They took Baby Brick to the fair.
These are the prizes
that Baby Brick won!
But still Mr and Mrs Brick
were worried.

They could not do their work.
They got things wrong
with the houses they built.

At last Mr and Mrs Brick
put Baby Brick in her push-chair.

They got on a bus.

They went on a train.

They sailed on a ship.

They rode on a camel –
and went to see Great Uncle Brick.

Great Uncle Brick was the most famous
builder in the Brick family.
He built houses all over the world.

"Our baby does not build,"
said Mr Brick.
"She knocks things down!"
Mrs Brick said.
Great Uncle stopped work
and took his hat off.
He looked at the baby.
Then he looked at Mr and Mrs Brick.
"What this baby needs is a little
brother," he said.

"It will take her mind off
knocking things down!"

So the next year Mr and Mrs Brick
had another baby.
And was *that* the answer?
Yes, it was!
This is the house
that Baby Brick built
for the new Baby Brick.

And this!   And this!

After that Mr and Mrs Brick
were very happy.
"Now we *do* have another builder
in the family," they said.
"All our worries are over!"

But were all their worries really over?
No, they were not.
This is the house
that the new Baby Brick . . .

. . . knocked down!